AF269085

DEAR
Future Husband
ANGEL DEVLIN

Chapter One

ELLA

We'd only just seemed to have had Christmas and New Year's, but now Valentine's Day was approaching. The shops were bursting with cuddly bears holding hearts saying, 'I love you', and women were coming into our boutique getting measured for the perfect dress for their weekend away or date night. It was all so romantic, and I was oh so single.

Jodi came through the door carrying my hopes and dreams. Okay it was my daily latte from *Happ-BEANness,* the coffee shop next door, but it was heaven in a cup and woke me up enough so I could make and sell beautiful clothes all day long, so I wasn't far off.

Jodi and I ran a boutique called *Sew in Style*. Front of house were the garments themselves, some on mannequins and others on rails. The back of our counter went through to our workshop so we could be working when we weren't serving customers. We had an Art Deco vibe going through the boutique and specialized in evening wear. They were clothes for occasions, so lots of mother-of-the-bride outfits, prom dresses, that kind of thing. We did the occasional wedding dress but not standard ones; only if the bride wanted maybe a 1950's style swing dress or something a little different to the norm.

"So how are Casey and Audrina today?" I asked after my friends who worked next door.

She gazed into the distance for a moment as if daydreaming and then turned back to me. "Oh God, they are so happy and loved up. It's enough to make you throw up in your drink."

My interest piqued. "Really? I know Casey is with Jared now, but who's Audrina dating?"

"A guy called Tom. He works with Jared apparently. Seriously, they kept giggling to each other as they were talking. It's too much. They need to employ someone single and miserable to make customers like me feel better."

"And me." I sighed, picking up my latest romance book. "No boyfriend has ever brought me flowers like I read about. I want a true old-fashioned romantic relationship. Not swipe-right on Tinder."

A customer who had been looking through the rails turned around and caught our attention.

"Sorry to interrupt, but I couldn't help overhear. I saw a lady on morning television a couple of days ago who runs a dating agency and she does things the old-fashioned way. You send letters to the person she matches you up with."

Jodi pulled a face. "Handwritten letters? Who has time for that?"

But I was already picturing spritzing the one I was sending with my perfume.

"That sounds amazing. What was the lady's name? I must look into it."

The woman looked up while she thought. "Grace... now what was her surname? Ah, Graham, like the crackers."

"Grace Graham. Thank you so much. I shall research that later."

I ignored Jodi's eye roll.

The woman brought a dress up to the counter. "I'd like to take this please. Your dresses are amazing. I hope you both know how talented you are."

I beamed. "Thank you, and because of your recommendation about the dating lady, I'd like to give you a 10% discount today."

The woman held her hand up. "That won't be necessary. Oh, and while I'm here do you do international delivery? Only, I'm off to Dublin in March."

"Wow. Dublin in Ireland?" I asked.

She nodded. "Yes. Quite a change seeing as I've lived in New York all my life, but an opportunity came up that I couldn't refuse."

"Oooh, what is it?"

"Ella, that could be private." Jodi warned, elbowing me.

"Sorry." I bit my lip. "I just love stories about adventure and dreams coming true, that kind of thing."

The customer smiled. "I'm going over to be a personal assistant to a member of a rock band."

"Oh my god. Seriously? Which one?"

"I can't say at the moment. Part of my contract, but it's very exciting. I'm Harlow, by the way." She looked at Jodi and me. "So about international delivery?"

"Just for you we'd consider it," Jodi said. "I'm sure it would be astronomical postage though. There are probably boutiques in Dublin who'd love your custom."

Harlow shrugged. "Maybe. I know nothing about the place, other than they drink Guinness! Anyway, nice to meet you both. Good luck on the dating front," she added before she left the shop.

"She seemed nice. What a job, working for a rock band. Ella... Ella, are you listening to me at all?"

I looked up from my phone. "Oh sorry, I was looking up that woman, Grace Graham."

Jodi sighed. "I give up. I'll go do the outfit of the day and then I'm going to start on the orders. You'd better stay at the front today, your head's not in a concentrating mood."

She was right. My mind had already pictured the slew of romantic posts passing between myself and my mystery man. He of course, would turn out to be my perfect man and future husband. We may only meet in person on our wedding day...

"Your coffee's getting cold." Jodi nodded at it. She shook her head and walked into the back.

Jodi had thousands of followers on Instagram as she posted an 'outfit of the day'. They were often from our own store but sometimes something she'd have found at Goodwill or from a department store. With long, sleek dark hair and a tall slim figure honed by yoga, she had the model pose off to a fine art. She kept asking me to do the same thing, but so far I'd resisted as I was a little on the plump side, five feet four, was a little shy at times and my bobbed wavy red hair clashed with a lot of colors.

Sipping at my coffee, I sat on the stool behind the counter and fired up the laptop. I'd opened a stock screen and at the same time a browser page for investigating Grace Graham. It was time to find out what this dating agency was all about and how I could contact them. This could be my New Year's resolution. To be brave and search for love. I felt a little tickle of excitement in my tummy. Something that had been absent for a long time in anything outside of boutique business or my daily latte! It was a welcome feeling.

Browser open, I typed in **Grace Graham**. In the research results came up whattheheartwants.com. I clicked the link to find only a picture of a heart and the words:

Site under construction

Damn it.

Moving back to the search results, I found an online magazine article all about Grace, so I decided that was a good place to start to find out more about her and her agency.

Grace Graham has been matchmaking now for 'more years than she can remember'. Her agency in St. Louis, Missouri, 'What The Heart Wants' is best known for its practice of the matchmade couple sending at least three handwritten letters to each other before they meet or get in touch via electronic means.

"The letters go through me so they don't know who they are matched with and therefore can't cheat the system and get in touch with each other until after that third letter. What they write is up to them, but I always recommend they communicate from the heart about their hopes and dreams and what they are looking for out of life. After they have written their three letters, they let me know whether or not they want to meet and that's when I arrange their blind date."

The system has resulted in a surprising number of success stories and quite a few weddings. What does Grace think it is about her service that makes it so successful?

"It's taking the pressure off that initial 'getting to know each other stage'. No one has to bare their soul face-to-face to find that the other isn't interested in what they have to say."

And what about the fact that the 'pen-pals' don't see each other?

"I match them with the information they provide to me on their perfect match. If they also get along fantastically in their letters, then I find what that person looks like physically becomes less important."

But what about people who want to match with others online in the modern way?

"I'm moving with the times and I'm currently in the process of setting up a website and a modern system with an app! We can have both running side-by-side."

And has Grace found her own true love? At this point she laughs.

"I'm too busy finding love for everyone else. It's sad, but true. At the moment it makes my heart happy to match up other people. One day it might happen for me, but I'm in no rush as I love putting couples together. Work consumes me and I don't think it would be fair right now to ask a man to compete with that."

So there you have it. The irony in that in matching

up other people, this lovely lady has no time for love herself. If you're interested in any of her services contact Gracegraham@whattheheartwants.com.

I wanted to clap my hands together. Her matchmaking service sounded utterly amazing. So romantic. Just imagine writing a letter to someone who could end up being your future husband! Then when you had children you could show them the letters, and they could be saved for their children's children, 'Look how your ancestors got together; it was so romantic.' I was so overcome I clutched a hand to my chest. Looking behind me, I could see that Jodi was lost in her designs, enjoying her own feelings of joy. While she was otherwise engaged and not watching me, I quickly opened my email and began composing a message for Grace Graham.

To: Gracegraham@whattheheart-wants.com

From: Ellacassidy@yahoo.com

Date: January 11, 2019

Subject: Joining your dating agency

Good morning Ms/Miss Graham

My name is Ella Cassidy and I have been reading about your letter writing matchmaking service. I'm not sure if you cover New York City with you being based in St. Louis, but I am hoping this is the case. I'm single (obvs, although maybe you do get applications from cheating spouses!), and I'm a born romantic. The idea of meeting my future husband through your service and the art of letter writing appeals to my romantic soul!

Anyhow, I would be very grateful if you could furnish me with further details.
Many thanks and wishing you a lovely day!
Kind regards

Ella.

I read it back through and pressed send. Then I concentrated on work although I checked my email around 476 times that day to see if Grace responded, but she didn't. No doubt she was inundated with applications from people like me. But just as Grace liked to match couples together, I liked to match people with their perfect outfit, so my day was spent doing what I loved, with finding love on hold.

Chapter Two

ELLA

Carrying takeout, I entered my apartment and shouted for my roommate. "Finn, you'd better have set the table, I have dinner."

Finn Edwards was the cousin of my first roommate. She'd decided to go live with her boyfriend and transferred her tenancy to Finn. Thank God we got along. He was an untidy pig, but so was I, so what could have been a tricky situation was avoided by the fact we both lived like we needed to star in an episode of Hoarders. Finn never tidied up his books, DVDs, shoes, vinyl. I had pieces of material and part-projects everywhere. We kept the place relatively clean, but tidy we were not.

A door opened and Finn walked in to the hall dressed in pajama pants that slung low on his hips. I kept my eyes on his face, despite the fact the man was built. No way would I ever have made a move on my roommate. I loved where I lived and wouldn't have done anything to jeopardize that, even if at times, it was hard to not ogle him. Finn Edwards was a sex god with his dark, almost black, wavy short hair and eyes that matched. When he looked at me when he wanted something, he'd play on those puppy dog eyes, but if anything riled him, you'd see their piercing depths.

"I know I'm hot, but please close your mouth, there's a draft."

Having realized I'd been in a daydream, I rolled my eyes at him and continued through to our kitchen diner where I placed the takeout on the small table.

"Don't flatter yourself. Did you just get up, you lazy jerk?"

He rubbed his eyes. "Yeah, been staring at a laptop all day. Made me tired, so I quit early and went back to bed." Finn was a self-employed book editor and worked from home.

"It's okay for some."

"Oh give it a rest, you love your job." He took

plates out of the cabinets and set them down on the table, then pulled out some silverware from a drawer.

"Wine?"

"Wine, not?" I replied.

"Oh God, no, just no. That is so bad."

"Why are you grinning then?" I challenged him.

"Just being polite." He poured us a glass of wine each.

We sat down and opened the takeout cartons, selecting what we wanted and loaded our plates.

"So how was your day?" Finn asked me. We had quite the routine going when we were both home at mealtimes, which we were most days. I'd bring food home with me and Finn would set the table and then we'd catch up on our days. I looked forward to it. It was nice to not be lonely and to have some company before I either went out for the evening, or as I did more often than not, escaped to my room with a book while Finn sat on the sofa playing video games. He'd asked me to join him a few times, but gaming was not my thing.

"Really good. We sold quite a few things today, and... a customer told me about a dating agency. I decided to get brave and I contacted the woman who owns it."

Finn coughed on a noodle. "You did?"

I nodded while smiling. "I know. I actually did something toward getting a date, instead of just reading about love in my many romance novels." I sighed. "I'm waiting for an email back to see if I can be included because the woman is from St. Louis."

"Ah, you probably are out of area then." Finn went back to his food.

I checked my phone.

"Oh my god! She replied!" I started reading.

"Read it out loud. I want to know what she said," Finn half-yelled.

"Okay, calm down, Mr. Excitable."

I read on.

"Dear Ella. Thank you so much for your enquiry. I would be happy to set you up with a suitor. In the first instance please fill in the attached application form with all your details and send this back to me as soon as you are able. Along with this, please mail me your first letter. This should be an introductory letter telling your match a little about yourself so they can get to know you. I will read your letter to check it meets the standards of my agency. These rules can be found here and include the fact that no information can be included that would tell the other where you live and no photographs or other items can be exchanged. Then there's a link and an invoice."

"Probably be an eighty-year-old dude when the reveal happens," Finn said scornfully.

"As long as he's rich," I bit back.

"It's your life, but I think you're crazy. At least if you joined a regular site, you'd know what they looked like. How long do you have to write letters for?"

"We have to exchange three and then we can meet."

"What a ball ache."

"Finn, I don't know what you're getting all annoyed at. It's me that's doing it, not you. You could at least be encouraging that I'm finally trying to do something about my love life." I sat up straight quickly. "Hey, why don't you do it too?"

Finn folded his arms across his chest. "Yeah, not happening. I can get plenty of dates without paying some dumb agency." He finished his wine.

"Well, good for you because I can't."

There was a minute of silence while we both ate.

"I'm sorry, Ella. I'm being hesitant about it because I know how full of romance that head of yours is and I don't want you to get hurt. But you're right. You do deserve love. Go for it. What's there to lose? I'll tell you what. If you like, I'll read your letter through for you and give you my input from a guy's point of view. How's that sound?"

"Really? Would you? That would be so helpful."

"And as a thank you, you can empty the trash, and clean the wine glasses and silverware while I go play on the Xbox." He pushed back his chair. "Thanks, Cinder-ella."

"Jerk," I shouted at his retreating back.

After I'd finished the clearing up, I retired to my bedroom to write my letter. I decided to type it into the computer first and then handwrite it because otherwise it could take forever. I'd show Finn the printout and then once I had a man's view on it, I'd handwrite it. God, then I'd need to decide what to write it on. A notelet, a plain piece of paper? Would I be judged on what I sent it on? It was something else I needed to ask Finn. For now, I just had to concentrate on my opening letter and how to sound so amazing, he wanted to date me (and even maybe in the future marry me).

Dear Stranger (this doesn't sound right, ask Finn).

My name is Ella and I am writing you this letter in the hopes that we may share common interests and get to know each other a little better. If we get along after the three letters then hopefully we will already know that we are quite compatible? I do understand some might think it's a strange way to get to know someone in this modern day and age, but do you know what? I'm tired of the swipe right mentality and the loss of romance.

It was no good, I needed Finn in here as I went along. I jumped off the bed and stuck my head out into the hall.

"Fiiiinnnnnnn."

"What?"

"I need you."

"What for?"

"My love letter."

"Needs to sound more enticing than that."

I bit my bottom lip. He was being a dick.

"Fiiiinnnn. I need you in my bedroom."

I heard a thud and he came running to my door. My eyes watched his junk bounce about in his pants. I was such a perve.

"Well, why didn't you say so?"

I shook my head. "You're such a dufus. Come in and help me. I'm writing nonsense."

"Oh my god, I am actually going in a girl's bedroom. I'm so excited." Finn skipped in. I couldn't help but laugh.

He swung around to me in the doorway. "Where do you want me?" He wiggled his eyebrows.

I giggled. "Finn, I need you on the bed."

He flicked his hair and pouted. "I was hoping you would say that." He jumped on the bed and hutched up to the right near the wall, placing my laptop on his knee and reading. Then he looked up at me. "Dear God, Ella. If I received that I'd be looking for a bucket to vomit into."

"It's not that bad."

"You say the word romance to the guy in the first paragraph. You've lost him."

"I need romance in my life. If the guy doesn't then he's not for me."

Finn patted the side of the bed. "Come here, squirt. Look, you lead up to that. Maybe letter number two, but here you want the guy to write back, right? So he needs to know you've got great tits, and an ass to die for."

"Finn!"

Finn held up his hands. "Do you want my input, or not?"

I got on the bed and sat next to him. I'd never been this close to him before and the side of his body now touching mine was all warm and lovely. In fact, come to think of it, I'd never had a man in this bed. This was a first.

"You're the first man who's ever been in my bedroom," I blurted out.

"Seriously? Even when Lara was here?"

"Even then. My love life is like a desert—harsh and unyielding."

He laughed.

"Finn, it's not funny."

"Oh, sorry. I'm not laughing at that. It's just the people I edit for often spell it dessert instead, you know like after a main meal, and then it would be a harsh and unyielding dessert, like it's still frozen or something."

I looked at him blankly.

"You have to be there, I guess. It's little things like that which amuse me during my working day."

"Great, now back to me." I elbowed him.

"Ouch," he said, nipping my waist.

I tickled his neck to see if he was ticklish. Finn didn't move.

He wiggled his fingers close to me.

"Please don't." I started giggling.

"Oh my god. I haven't even tickled you and you're already laughing."

"I can't help it, I know what's coming."

He wiggled his fingers closer and the laptop wobbled precariously on his lap.

"Watch my laptop," I warned. "Now, back to work."

"Okay, let me try to type a combination of your stuff and what I would want to read. Don't kill the messenger, okay? If you don't like it, you're free to change it. Just let me do my thing."

"Fine. Go for it. I'll change it after."

"How do you know you won't keep it?"

"Lucky guess."

I watched as his fingers swept across the keys.

Hey there, I'm Ella!

This letter thing is crazy, right? But I'm game, if you are ;)

So first of three, I'll give you some quick details about me.

I'm single (obvs).

I'm twenty-five.

I have red hair (I know what you're thinking, but a girl never tells her secrets straight off).

"You can't put that!" I screeched.

"Yes, it's staying. It's flirty and shows you might be up for a future hook up. Anyway, are you a natural redhead?"

I flicked his ears. "A girl never tells her secrets straight off."

He pulled his tongue out at me and carried on.

My hobbies include fitness and partying.

"Finn, I come straight home from work most nights, unless I'm out with the girls, and the last time I went to a gym was about eight years ago."

"This gives the impression you have stamina and you're up for it."

"Is that all a guy wants to know? That I'll put out?"

"Basically, yes."

"Well, that's just tragic. I'm not sure I want to do this anymore if I can't send the romantic letter I want to send."

I sat back against my headboard and tears welled,

threatening to spill over. I didn't want someone who wanted a quick fuck. I wanted romance.

Finn looked at me and deleted his whole letter. We were back to a blank screen.

"Why did you do that?"

He shrugged. "You're right. You're trying this because you want something different. So, go for it. But don't write what you did before either. Fully go for it. Write the dream. Write what you want and then if it doesn't work out, at least you'll know you gave it everything you had."

I stared at him. "Finn, I had no idea you could be so profound."

"There's a lot you don't know about me. I have hidden depths." He farted. "That came from one of them."

I grabbed my laptop and dashed out of the room back to the living room, screaming that he was a dirty pig to fart on my bed and he'd never be allowed in there again.

His laughter echoed down the hall as he returned to his own room. Jerk.

Heading to the kitchen, I poured myself a glass of wine. Then I returned to the living room and settled down on the sofa, resting against a comfy cushion. After taking a huge gulp of the red and enjoying the burst of berries on my tongue, I placed the glass on the coffee table and picked up my laptop, placing it on my knee. I decided I was going for it. I would write what the hell I wanted and if the guy didn't reply, he wasn't for me. In fact—I thought about what Finn said—I would potentially scare my could-be suitor right from the off. Flexing my fingers, I started my letter:

Dear Future Husband

Also, I decided I'd make Finn read my letter in the morning. He'd die! Feeling energized, I carried on.

Still reading? Not made you run a mile, or burn this letter on a pyre? Congrats, we might have a connection.
I'm Ella. I'm twenty-five, a redhead, and I'm a dressmaker. My love life has been virtually non-existent for the past year. A customer spoke of Grace Graham and What the Heart Wants and I

decided why not go for it? Try a different way of meeting someone. I love the idea of sending letters: sending a letter to you; someone matched for me, yet anonymous. Whereas in real life I'm kinda shy, here I can open myself up across the pages and if I blush, well, you won't see it, will you!

I don't exercise unless you count lifting a glass of wine to my mouth. I love watching old movies and they don't have to be romantic! I spend far too much time reading magazines and watching TV shows about fashion. Fashion is my passion.

My ideal date would be a stroll in Central Park, or even maybe a carriage ride, followed by a lovely meal in a restaurant.

I have a loving family including my parents and a younger sister. They live far enough away to not be a nuisance, but close enough for us to see each other regularly.

Music wise I love Taylor Swift. I'm sorry! Maybe I should have put that at the beginning. I can

already see you groaning about my loving girlie pop! But I can't help myself, she's inspirational to me.

I'll leave my first letter here, short and sweet. Hoping you managed to read to the end without requiring a bucket to vomit in.

Love, Ella.

I read it back through and happy with what I'd typed, I went into my now fart-free bedroom and chose a notelet with an illustration of a table in a café bearing a steaming cup of coffee on the front. It reminded me of HappBEANness. Back in the living room, I handwrote the note using my best pen and handwriting. Placing it in an unsealed envelope, I put that and the application form in a larger envelope addressed to Grace. Before I could change my mind, I got my shoes and coat on and headed to the mailbox.

It felt ceremonious as I stood before the mailbox. I kissed the back of the envelope and let it go. My love life was in the hands of fate.

Back in the apartment, I printed a copy off and folded it. I scrawled across a blank part:

Finn, this is what I sent in the end and it's too late, I mailed it already! Ella.

I posted it under his door.

Chapter Three

FINN

I wasn't asleep when I heard footsteps hovering outside my door and then a piece of paper came through underneath. Waiting until Ella's feet padded down to her own room, I got up from my bed and picked up the paper. I read the words she was writing to another man. A stranger. I realized I was scrunching the paper up in my fist, I was so pissed.

We'd lived together for over a year now. A year of blue balls, that's what I'd termed it. My cousin told me straight that I wasn't to view Ella as another conquest and nail her, as I needed a place where I could settle more permanently, to leave my manslut persona behind. I'd not even slept with that many people. I just ended up with a reputation after a bad break-up and a vengeful ex.

Anyhow, when I first met Ella, I thought I was safe, that she wasn't my type. But then she grew on me like some type of fungus. What's a sexy kind of fungus? Does one exist? Because once I started noting the little mannerisms, like how when thinking she'd suck on her bottom lip slightly while going 'hmmm', my cock decided it wanted to sink into her womanly depths. She was a grower, was Ella. Rather like my cock right now while it was thinking of her. However, once I started scanning the note, the actual words she'd sent to another man, my boner soon withered and died.

Dear Future Husband?
Dear FUCKING FUTURE HUSBAND?
What the actual fuck?

A dude was going to get this and run far, far away. A cold fear clamped around my guts. But what if they didn't? What if they thought she was their ideal woman and wrote back? They either may read within the note a naivete and decide to play on that, or else they could be a wimp who wanted a little wifey at home that would please mama, but their buck teeth and acne-ridden face couldn't procure one in the real world. My thoughts were not PC and were going to have me on a one-way-trip to Hell, but she was writing letters to another guy, hoping one might marry her, so I was halfway there already.

Was she blind?

She fucking lived with me and I walked around half-naked trying to get her to notice me.

Dude, it was time to accept she wasn't interested. She wanted to date some fucking romantic nerd who was going to rock up on a white horse, go down on bended knee, and impregnate her with a million cherubic cheeked babies and keep her in comfort in her white picket fence house.

This was not acceptable.

I fired up my own laptop and found the details of this Grace Graham.

My own options were now running out, so I'd have to act fast.

Chapter Four

ELLA

I had a great beaming smile on my face the whole morning while I got showered and breakfasted ready for my working day. Finn, on the other hand, was banging around the place like he'd been possessed by Satan himself.

He sat at the kitchen table, his cereal bowl hitting the mat, and milk sloshing over the side.

"What on earth is going on with you this morning?" I asked.

"Didn't sleep well."

That explained everything. Sometimes Finn had bouts of insomnia and when he did, he was a right moody bastard.

I came up behind him and began to massage his shoulders. "Are you all tense? Maybe if you calmed down, you'd begin to feel sleepy. At least you can get your head down for an hour, being self-employed."

He shrugged away from me. "Well, not really, because I can't exactly work while I'm asleep, can I? Everyone seems to think self-employment means not working at all." He spooned a mouthful of cereal into his mouth.

"Wow. You grumpy fucker. I'm off to work and I'll leave you to it. Don't take it out on the apartment. I hope when I'm home you've changed your attitude because I don't deserve to be on the receiving end of it." I picked up my purse from the back of a chair.

His face relaxed from its previous snarl and he looked at me with doe-eyes.

Not the doe-eyes.

I can't resist the doe-eyes.

I needed to look away, but I couldn't. They were hypnotizing me.

"I'm sorry, Ella. You're right. I shouldn't be taking it out on my girl. Come here."

"No."

"Please. I want to give you an apology hug and a

'see you later, have a nice day' hug all rolled into one."

"Why should I? I just tried to help you relax and got attitude for it."

A pout appeared.

Now we had a pout and doe-eyes.

The big guns were out. Oh and now he was holding out his arms. The big guns really were out. Popping from his upper arms. God, I wanted to squeeze them.

Doe-eyes. Pout. Guns. Full ammo ahead.

My body walked me forward toward him, the betraying bastard. His arms came around me and he squeezed me.

"Sorry, my Ella. Have a lovely day at work. Hey, I'll grab the takeout tonight and some wine, okay? My apology for being an ass."

I looked down at him. "Will it be pizza?"

"Can be."

"Will there be ham and pineapple?"

He groaned. "You're killing me here, Ella. Yes, I'll get you some goddamn ham and pineapple and I'll try not to retch while you eat it."

"Apology accepted. Now let me go. Some of us have to travel to their place of work."

"It's like five minutes walk away!"

I gave him side-eye. "Quit while you're ahead or I'll make you eat a piece of pineapple later."

He let me go.

It was only once I was out of the door that I realized I didn't ask him if he'd had chance to read my letter.

It was my morning to collect our coffees from HappBEANness. I pushed open the door and found the place was bustling. It was only 9am!

Casey spotted me and pointed to a seat, so I took it. A few minutes later she walked over with our regular orders and a paper bag. "Two blueberry and apple muffins."

"Oooh, my favorite. Thank you. How come you're so busy? It's amazing, but it's not usually like this."

"We advertised our drink for Valentine's. A special ginseng tea, along with a heart-shaped ginger cookie for a special price and it was featured in a weekly women's magazine! People are coming from far and wide to sample them. I'm making the most of it while it lasts." She looked over at the counter. "I'd better get back or Audrina will start whining."

I passed her the money for our drinks and goodies, left with a wave to Audrina, and walked next door into our very quiet shop. The difference was marked, but I knew which I preferred. I like our quiet ambience and bespoke service, versus the chaos next door, although thank goodness they were there to keep me nicely loaded with caffeine.

Jodi was already working on a custom order. "Morning. Oh, thank God for coffee. Coffee doesn't turn up boring as hell."

Jodi had been on a date last night.

"That good, eh?"

"Let's just say if I could be bothered with the whole letter writing thing, I'd be tempted to give your idea a shot, but for now I'll stick to Match and my mother's erstwhile matchmaking attempts." She took a sip of coffee. "How are you getting on anyway? Did you hear back from that woman?"

"Heard back, application filled in, first letter written, and all mailed."

"Boy, you don't hang around, do you?"

"Well, Grace needs to read it, select someone to match me with and then the mail service can take up to five days, so I wanted a head start."

"So what did you put in your letter?"

I looked at my feet.

"Ella, what did you do?"

Straightening up my posture I looked Jodi straight in the eye. "I wrote a letter to my future husband. I actually addressed it to that. Dear Future Husband. And although I feel embarrassed telling you, I don't regret it. I'm going for it, for love. I'm all in."

Jodi laughed. "You don't think you could have started with Dear My Valentine, seeing as we're on the run up to the supposed most romantic day of the year?"

I lifted my shoulders. "I'd had wine."

The doorbell rang and in walked Finn.

"What are you doing here? Did I forget something?"

He shook his head. That gorgeous hair was flopping around. I wondered how soft it felt.

"No. I decided it was time to get that suit I'm always saying I'll have made to measure. Only Valentine's Day is coming up and I might have a hot date. You know, one where I have to dress up in my finest."

"Ooooh," Jodi said. "Do tell, because my Valentine's is likely to be spent with Ben & Jerry and my pajamas. Who and where?"

"Couldn't possibly say who as I haven't actually

asked them out yet and I don't know where because I only thought of it last night and so I need to look around."

"But you want a suit even though you don't actually have a date or anywhere to go? You get weirder." I rolled my eyes at him while trying not to think too hard about why I was acting snippy with him about it.

"Says the person mailing letters addressed to her future husband to strange men."

"Okay, okay, you two. You're both weird," Jodi interrupted. "Comes to something when I'm the most well-adjusted after a date set up by my mother went awry. Anyway, why didn't you just let Ella measure you at the apartment?"

"I'm not having her anywhere near my inside leg." Finn looked at Jodi in horror. "She might use it as an excuse to molest me."

"In your dreams," I shot back. "Anyway, I wouldn't go anywhere near your lower end with the rancidness of the fart you did last night."

"Are all customers treated this shabbily?" Finn addressed Jodi.

"Come on through to the back, Finn. Let's get you measured up." Jodi was doing her best not to grin, but I could see the telltale signs. She thought the sun shone out of Finn's ass and couldn't understand why I hadn't 'accidentally' sleepwalked into his bed.

It'd crossed my mind believe me. But no, we were roommates, and he was great to live with. I didn't want to ruin that. Plus, he didn't think of me that way at all. He treated me like one of his dudes, hence letting rip right at the side of me.

No. All I needed to do now was wait for Grace's magic matchmaking skills and the mail service.

Saturday, January 12, 2019

After waiting every morning for the mail, a package finally arrived from What The Heart Wants. I actually squealed out loud.

"Keep it down. Me and the boys had a big night last night," Finn yelled from his room.

I picked up the mail and tiptoed into the kitchen, placing the package on the table. I was dying to tear the envelope open, but I wanted to do it properly, with a bit of ceremony, so I fixed the machine to make me a coffee, brought my drink to the table and sat down.

I tore open the envelope.

There was a letter with the 'What The Heart Wants' letterhead and two envelopes, one plain white, one pink.

I read the official letter.

Dear Ella

I must start with an apology.

As you know I do everything by hand, but I am in the midst of putting some of my business online and automated. My assistant got confused with your application and so as well as the person I physically matchmade you up with, she had your perfect partner chosen on the computer too.

It left me in a bit of a quandary as to what to do for the best, so in the end I decided I would send your details to both suitors. Both of their letters are enclosed. It is entirely up to you whether you choose to correspond with one or both of them for the duration of the three letters.

My heartfelt apologies and I am refunding half of your fee as a goodwill gesture.

Hoping you find your perfect match. You have double the chance of everyone else!

Love, Grace.

I sat back straight on my seat, astonished. I had two. TWO potential husbands? So one of them must have been sent my letter electronically I guessed.

I opened the plain white envelope and sure enough there was a handwritten letter, but one that had been scanned through an electronic system. I placed it down and picked up the pink envelope. I noticed it had a smell to it. Picking it up, I sniffed it and realized it was my favorite men's aftershave. It was a really popular one. Finn wore it and so did Audrina's brother (who was also Casey's boyfriend). It put this guy in the lead for me so far. I began reading.

Dearest Future Wife
Thank you for your recent letter. I decided to wholeheartedly embrace your idea of conversing with you as a potential future partner!
Why not?
I'm Gavin, I'm twenty-eight, and I work in a library. I adore literature. Poetry, fiction, biography. You name it, I'm a fan. I do also enjoy movies, but I'd rather read the book if it's an adaptation.
Exercise wise, a stroll in the park sounds good. I

do like to visit the gym a few times a week to keep myself in peak condition, but I also love fresh air.

I too have both my parents, along with an annoying younger brother who is the same size as me in clothes and calls around to my apartment when I'm not there and 'borrows' them.

My ideal date would be a meal somewhere very romantic, maybe with a scenic backdrop, soft music and candlelight.

Is it too forward to say that I hope one day to be a father? I'd like at least one child but as many as makes my future wife happy. I hope I've not scared you away with that comment, but we seem to be saying we'll give these letters our all! Music wise I like classical. If you play Taylor Swift, I shall forgive you (and wear noise cancelling headphones).

Hope to hear back from you soon.

Gavin.

Taking a long sip of my coffee, I read the letter through a second time and a third, trying to commit its contents to memory. I then went through it slowly line-by-line as if more about him would appear from my in-depth explorations.

I placed it down on the table almost reverently, not wanting to get any marks on it, and I picked up the second letter–the scanned one–and began reading.

Hi, Mrs. X!
Fantastic to receive your letter and for us begin the process of getting to know each other. I've decided to keep my name a secret until after letter three. I hope you don't mind. Just thought it might add to the mystery. So you can call me Mr. X.
I'm 6 feet tall, have dark hair, dark eyes and a body built for sin.
You can play Taylor Swift. We can fuck to it.
My ideal date would be to come pick you up from your apartment. I'd be in a dinner suit and you'd be in a sheer, silky gold dress with a deep 'V' at the back showing a little curve just above your ass. We'd have had these reservations for ages, for a high-end establishment, and yet we'd risk missing the reservation as I pushed you against the wall claiming your mouth with mine. My left hand would be fisted in your hair, tipping your head back so that I could trail kisses down your neck and across your collar-

bone, eliciting goose bumps and shivers. My right hand would grasp the material of your gown and hitch it up above your hip where I'd find you weren't wearing panties, which you'd tell me was because you didn't want a visible panty line, but I would know it's because you're horny as fuck and your wet pussy would confirm that as I dipped a finger in that slick heat.

I noticed my mouth was ajar. I couldn't believe what I was reading. Yet, despite the fact a small part of me was saying throw the letter away, it was rude and impolite; the other part of me wanted to read on, and to be honest my own pussy was cheering on the imagined scenario. So I carried on reading.

You arch against my finger as I curl it in just the right way. Bringing that finger to my lip, I suck on it, my eyes staring into your hooded gaze. I make a joke about us leaving now and you pull me back to you, kissing me with an intensity that has me loosening my suit pants there and then. My cock nudges against you, accepted into your slick heat and I thrust deep inside, listening to your groans and your little mewls as

I push you against the wall again and again. My finger returns to find your nub and I rub against it, creating the friction you need so that along with my cock, you can't control yourself and you scream my name as I take you over the edge, your pussy milking my cock of every last drop. We sink against the wall, our foreheads together for a moment or two, and then we clean up and grab a cab, arriving fashionably late for our reservation. All the way in the cab we give each other knowing looks and as we apologize for our late arrival, we know we don't mean it. We also know we won't stay around for dessert because we'll be too eager to get back home for a repeat performance.
X.

That was it. He told me relatively little about himself, just about how he would fuck me. I was so confused. And horny.

Confused and horny.

I read it again. Oh my, I was so wet. I needed to get myself off.

Taking the letter, I went back to my bedroom. Snores were coming from Finn's room so I knew I wouldn't be disturbed.

God, I was disgraceful. But it was such a hot scenario!

Climbing into bed, I held the letter in one hand and stuck my other under the covers and down my pajama bottoms. Unsurprisingly, I found myself wet and ready.

I began to read the letter again. Then I discarded it on the bed as I closed my eyes, letting my imagination take over.

My fingers swept my clit as I imagined the mysterious Mr. X having dragged up my gown to find me wanting and wet.

I placed two fingers together and imagined they were his cock, pushing them inside my wet core and thrusting my hips upward.

Though I was so very close, something was missing, and I realized I wanted to be against the wall, acting out this fantasy as close to reality as I could get.

Climbing out of bed almost in a sexual frenzy, I stood against my bedroom wall, pulling my pajama top up a little so I could feel the cold of the wall against my back, imagining it was the bare flesh exposed by my low-cut dress. I closed my eyes and fucked my fingers. My back pushed against the wall as my excitement grew. I placed a finger from the other hand against my clit and rubbed, exactly as the letter said. Then I was coming—hard—over my hand, and a groan escaped me. I was powerless to stop it because I was coming harder than I ever remembered coming before. I felt like a puddle of goo and I headed for my bed, closing my eyes and letting sleep overcome me.

Chapter Five

FINN

I heard the clatter of the mail and then what sounded like an elephant running to the front door. For a small woman, Ella sure made a lot of noise. She'd been like this for days now. Like an Olympic athlete to the front door, only to usually moan with disappointment when there was nothing there. Then she was grumpy as fuck.

But this morning it would appear the hoped-for mail had arrived as she squealed like a practicing opera singer. I'd had a heavy night last night with my friends and it pierced my skull. I told her to keep it down. After that I heard her go to the kitchen and put on the coffee machine. There was silence so I knew she was reading. I imagined her reaction to her mail, and I waited for her to scream out about disgusting pigs, but she didn't. I fell back to sleep.

Glancing at the clock, I saw I'd only been out about twenty minutes or so. I felt like something had woken me up. Then I heard it again. A weird noise against the wall separating my room from Ella's. What the fuck was she doing? It sounded like something was brushing the wall. She was never cleaning at this time in the morning? She knew I'd got a freaking hangover. Maybe it was a stress reaction to the letter? You see I may have contacted Grace Graham and asked if I could send some mail myself as a little experiment. The woman herself had called me and we had had a little chat about what I wanted to do. So I knew exactly what Ella had received this morning because I had written that explicit letter myself. It was everything I wanted to do to Miss Ella Cassidy and couldn't.

I was going to show Ella that you couldn't know who your match was from a letter. That you could be writing to absolutely anybody. That the person could be right in front of your nose, but you'd believe they were some other person from what they wrote to you. I was surprised Grace agreed to it, given she was supposed to make the matches, not have them dictated to her, but she said she felt it was worth trying. Maybe her business wasn't doing as well as she made out?

I heard a groan. The unmistakable sound of Ella coming. I'd heard her before. She might think she was quiet, but the walls were thin. Then her feet padded away from the wall.

Had she come against the wall?

What was she doing?

Then a thought zapped across my mind, the scene in glorious Technicolor. *No!* Had she just acted out the scenario in my letter? The thought itself was enough that I had to wrap my hand around my girth and jerk myself off.

Ready to hit the shower, I woke myself up with a relatively cool one, wrapped a towel around my waist, and headed back to my room. Soft snores came from Ella's room. Bless her, even her snores were cute. I very gently opened her door a little to see her curled up under her covers, mouth open. She looked so peaceful. I also saw that the letter I sent had fluttered onto the floor.

She really had got off to it!

Once I was dry, I made some fresh coffee and saw that the other letter was discarded on the kitchen table. Hmm, she may say she wanted hearts and flowers, but it would appear that Ella was most attracted to the thought of hot, rampant sex.

Result!

Chapter Six

ELLA

When I woke up and realized where I was, back in bed after a rampant masturbation session, my cheeks flushed with an incinerating heat. I showered and dressed and made my way to the kitchen because I needed another coffee, and now I needed something to eat too because it was past lunchtime and I was ravenous.

Finn was sitting at the kitchen table, the letter addressed to 'my dearest wife' at the side of him.

"I don't suppose you haven't read it?"

He lifted his hands. "You left it out on the kitchen table. I'm a nosy fucker. Course I read it.

Then I puked, rinsed my mouth, and came back to the kitchen table for more coffee."

I pulled my lips into a saccharine smile. "Ha ha."

"So you like this then? Is this what you were looking for in your ideal man?"

Even though surprisingly I was more taken in by the 'I would fuck you' letter, there's no way I could back down now. Plus, the guy did sound nice. I'd already decided to write back to both of them. I may as well see where both got me.

"Absolutely. Later this evening I will settle down on the couch and pen my next letter to Gavin, my potential future husband."

Finn mock shivered. "God, it just seems so creepy. He could weigh six-stone and be riddled by acne."

"And if it's true love, I'd love him anyway," I protested, even though we both knew I couldn't stomach those pimple-popper clips on the internet and so would be likely to vomit all over my potential future skin-challenged husband.

Finn stood up.

"Where are you going? You've not finished your coffee."

"I was just off to find my violin."

"Fuck you."

He winked which made my cheeks heat again, this time in a cold fury.

I poured myself a coffee and picked up my letter again. "So is your head better now?"

"Yeah, I just needed a few extra hours in bed. All good now, or it will be after this coffee. I was thinking of making some bacon and egg. Fancy it?"

My stomach growled in appreciation.

"I'll take that as a yes."

While he stood cooking, Finn told me about his drinking escapades. He didn't mention any women, but I'm sure there would have been some hanging around. Hanging off his every word, like he was a god.

"So what are your plans today?" he asked me.

"I'm going to make a dress," I told him. "I'm going to pop out for some material and then do some prep."

"Can't you leave work at home for once? We could catch a movie or something."

"No, I really want to make this dress."

"There's a classic with Doris Day on this afternoon."

"It's in my head. I need to make it."

"It's a mild day. We could walk around Central Park?"

"I'm making the dress."

"Fuck, it must be something sensational if you're all consumed. What's so important about it?"

"Err." How could I tell him it featured in a fantasy in a letter he didn't know I received?

"I dreamed it. You know when I went back to bed. I was so tired and now I'm so glad I decided to catch a couple more hours because this dress is going to be amazing, and it's not work, because it's for me. I need to go get some gold silk or satin like material. It's a dress for an elegant evening out. One I don't even have planned, Finn, but I just have a burning desire to make it. I can clearly picture it in my mind."

"Well, I wouldn't want to get in the way of your burning desires. I'll take off and hit the gym, and then I'll do some work myself. Probably go to Happ-BEANness. I'll take my laptop out with my gym bag. Might as well get ahead on the work while you go all boring and obsessed on your latest project."

"Say hi to Casey and Audrina for me."

"I'll be sure to tell them how I offered you an afternoon of my company and I was turned down for an afternoon of dressmaking."

He handed me my bacon and eggs and just for a second I felt guilty. Finn offered to do the things he read in the letter that I liked, and I turned him down for a fantasy lover. But the lover could become a reality and Finn was the actual fantasy, so I just needed to stick to my plans.

Later that night I began to write my second letters.

Dear Future Husband (I know you're Gavin but I'm sticking with my original opening line!)

It was so lovely to hear from you.

No, I don't think it's too early to tell me you'd like to be a father. I did address my first letter to my future husband! I think it's important from the outset to state the things we hope for, otherwise we're not really getting to know each other, but rather just scratching the surface, aren't we?

I also would like children. I don't know how many. Maybe start with one and see how that goes, hahaha. I'd also like to have pets. A dog or a cat maybe. Not sure which I'd want first, the pets or the babies!

I'm imagining you quoting poetry at me in the park having read how learned with literature you are. That does sound romantic. Maybe a picnic and along with the sandwiches we take a few books and talk about how wonderful the prose is while we enjoy some good food and maybe even a sneaky bottle of wine?

I also like the sound of the candlelit dinner. We could have the classical music playing in the background as I don't think my Taylor Swift would do much for the ambience!

Moving things along in this letter, I currently live in an apartment, but long-term I see myself in a home with a small yard for my child/children to play in. It would need a guest room also for my dressmaking as I currently have things dotted around all over the apartment (which does my roommate's head in, as they may have trod on a rogue pin once or twice!).

It would need to be close to my business that I run with a friend also.

I suppose we'd better talk about our more unsavory qualities this time around. I must admit that I love eating the smelliest cheese there is (another thing my poor roommate has to put up with). As I said I leave dressmaking things around, mainly because I become entirely consumed by the process. It's such a passion. Everything else seems to fade into the background when I'm designing. That's another not ideal quality for any partner in my life but it's how it is. I love my work. But I'm totally aware that in the future when I have a family I might need to be a little less obsessed by my work.

I'm told I snore a little (but only lightly).

I really have to have the seat in the bathroom left down. It being left up drives me insane. In my future home I would love my own bathroom, just for me, that I could fill with scented candles and make a total girl zone.
Best, Ella.

Then it was time to write back to the other one. I couldn't believe that these had to be read by Grace before she mailed them on. I'd bet her memoirs were going to be something spectacular!

Dear Mr. X

Well, your letter was something I wasn't expecting.

All I'm going to say this time around is I'm making the dress.

Ella xo

I smiled a self-satisfied smile. I'd managed to convey a huge message in just those few lines without having to say a single dirty word myself. It was a tease of a letter.

I handwrote both letters out on plain white paper and placed them in white envelopes this time, and then put those in a large envelope which I addressed to Grace. Then I popped out to mail them. With up to five days for it to reach Grace and then her having to pass on the letters and the reply, I had a long wait ahead. Letter writing was proving to be quite the delayed gratification.

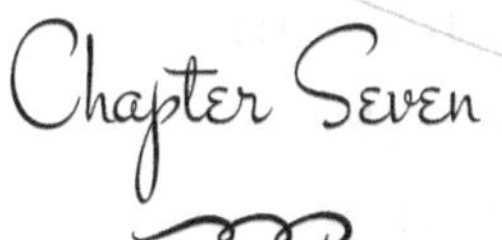

Chapter Seven

FINN

I'd spent the day keeping out of Ella's way. When I got home, she was consumed by her dressmaking. As I'd learned by now to not go anywhere near her, or even attempt to talk to her, while she was in the midst of a creative process, I called one of my friends and arranged to go bowling and then for drinks again afterward.

When I returned later that evening, Ella had gone to bed but she'd left out her laptop. I knew her passcode to her Word docs as she used the same damn thing for anything. The name of her old pet cat and then just added a number after it every time she had to update, so Tiddles8 got me through to her drafted out letters, and gave me advance notice of what Grace would pass on to me.

I had to admit, I'd been hoping for some jerking off material, but her letter was well-played. Now it was a case of waiting for Grace to send it onto me (in a brown unmarked envelope so Ella wouldn't get suspicious) and then I could write back again.

God, this waiting was torture.

Chapter Eight

ELLA

Wednesday, January 23, 2019

The mail hit the mat just as I was on my way out of the door. I scooped it up, popped it in my purse and made my way to work.

"Well?"

"Give me chance to get my coat off, will you?"

"You've got replies, haven't you? What do they say?"

I'd filled Jodi in on everything and I think she was almost as excited as I was.

"It only dropped through on my way out, so I've not had chance to open them yet. You go get the coffees while I actually get set for doing some work around here and then I'll open them."

Jodi grabbed her purse and didn't even bother with her jacket. "There'd better not be a queue, is all I'm saying. If there is, I'm declaring a state of emergency and pushing to the front."

It was cruel but I'd deliberately hoped there was a queue because I wanted to read my letters myself before I shared them with Jodi.

Both this time were in plain white envelopes, so I didn't know which I'd open first. I ripped open the first envelope and found a letter from Gavin. Did my insides just drop a little in disappointment that it wasn't the horny Mr. X's letter? I was disappointing myself with my physiology. Maybe I just generally needed to get laid more?

Dearest future wife,

Well it sounds like we already have two perfect dates lined up. Firstly, a trip to the park where we shall read poetry and drink champagne. (You said wine but maybe champagne is more roman-

tic, and we could also eat strawberries?) Then again maybe you don't like champagne and that's why you said wine. Either is fine with me! Then secondly, we can eat by candlelight with classical music in the background. Afterwards I feel it's only fair if we go somewhere that plays Taylor Swift so you can have a singalong or a dance.

Then somehow between these dates and a suitable period of time we will move onto the new home, pets, and children! Feels a little strange saying this here, but everything is in full working order, though you can never know if you are firing the right shots, if you get my drift!

I'm allergic to cats, so we'd have to go adopt the cutest little puppy as soon as we got our new home. Then we could work on the babies...

You'd definitely need your own workspace so that you could expand your business if required. After all, if we had small children, maybe you'd like to do some work from home. Although I must confess I'm not the neatest person myself.

Still, I don't think the idea of pins in my feet is one that features in my future fantasies!

I would like to write my own books one day. Maybe it's a dream, but seeing as we're talking about our ideal future, mine would be to be able to work from home writing, and that way I can take my fair share of the childminding and dogsitting duties and support your career.

My bad points. Hmm, let me see...

I can be a real grumpy ass after I've been out for the night. I think it's because my drinking days are coming to an end. Could I be getting too old???!!!!

Sometimes I break wind and it smells. (I'm guessing you do too). I promise to try to walk out of the room if I know one's coming, but sometimes they sneak out. And I might laugh, because I'm a guy, and we do this, even though it annoys women. (Sorry, but I felt we were at the stage of warts and all!!)

I can be jealous. Not to the point of psychotic.

But if a woman is mine, I can be a bit alpha. I'm not possessive in the sense of how some men won't allow their girlfriend to go out, but if a man talks to her, I might have to tell him to back off—you know do a bit of male postulating.

Hoping none of the above has put you off, and that you write our third letter!
Your (potential) future husband xo

Jodi came through the door clutching our drinks. I startled guiltily.

"You bitch! You started without me. What's it say?"

I exchanged a coffee for the letter. She placed both her coffee and my letter on the counter and sat on the stool behind before picking the letter back up.

I watched her face as she took in all the content. She looked up at me.

"Do you not find it disturbing that this guy knows all your hopes and dreams and you are both talking to each other like you might actually get together, when there could be no sexual chemistry between you at all? What if he's given your details and after you meet on the date, you can't stand him, and then he becomes a complete psycho. Like Joe in YOU. Oh my god, what if he kills me? Or kills Finn. Actually, yeah, he'd be more likely to kill Finn, see him as a threat, and then hopefully he'd be caught before he worked his way around to me. Phew."

"Okay, yes, let's address how crazy Gavin might be..." I made a cuckoo noise and pointed to Jodi.

She shook her head. "You can call me crazy, but you might wanna address the security Grace employs in all this before you meet him. Perhaps you could have Finn wait somewhere as a bodyguard. He's ripped enough."

"Yeah, actually, that's not a bad idea. And he'll totally go for it. Not because he's concerned for my safety, but because he's a nosy bastard who will be dying for it to be a Mr. Bean lookalike so he can fall about laughing and prove that I'm a romantic idiot."

"Romantic? Basically, the guy told you if he farts when you meet, he'll warn you first and leave the room."

I burst out laughing. "Well, at least he'll warn me, not like Finn!"

"Now open the other letter. I'm not sure coffee was a good idea. We might get too hot. Shall I go back next door for two ice-teas?"

"I'm reading it first. Then I will pass it to you."

"God, you're cruel. Well, hurry up."
I tore open the letter.

Dear, Mrs. X!

Well played! There I was hoping for a letter full of your deepest, darkest fantasies, and instead you tease me with the information you are making the dress from those fantasies.

So, all I'm going to say is I have my suit... and I made reservations.

For Valentine's Day.

Our letters should be finished by then.

Be my Valentine (and my potential future wife).
X

Ps what's happening when we skip dessert and get back home? If you tell me that, I'll tell you what I have planned for the next morning...

Otherwise my final letter will just say what time

I'm picking you up (when I have your address of course).

"What is it? I'm guessing it's not good with the look of disappointment on your face."

I passed over the letter.

"Oh, well played, Mr. X. This one is definitely a match for you."

"How can you say that? The only thing I know about this one really is how he'll seduce me."

"It's how he knows exactly the way to push your buttons. I love it. You thought your letter was so clever and now he's put the ball right back in your court."

"And we kinda wasted a letter each."

"Not really. I think it's flirty. Now you need to think of what you're going to send back. Your deepest, darkest fantasies. That's what he wants. Shall I get a pen?"

"No!" I protested. "There's no way I'm writing my sexual fantasies down in my place of work with my best friend present. Jeez. I shall drink an entire bottle of wine tonight and do it then."

The door dinged open and in walked Finn.

"Oh, the very man. Ella needs you," Jodi announced.

"She does?" Finn said, eyes wide.

"Yes, for Valentine's Day. You doing anything?"

Finn actually blushed! I didn't think I'd ever seen him embarrassed before. "Well, does that mean—"

"She needs you to be her bodyguard. She has a date with one of these suitors. There'll probably be a date with the other one too. We need to know they aren't psychopaths, so can you sit in a corner somewhere to make sure she stays alive?"

"Jodi! The guy just came through the door, and you've ambushed him. I was going to ask him later."

She grimaced. "Oh, sorry. It's not my fault my love life is crap and I'm excited over yours."

Finn looked entirely uncomfortable. Did he think when she said Valentine's, I wanted him to take me out? I bet he did. He looked so unsure then. Not like the Finn I know.

"Sure, I can do that no problem. I'd not sorted out my date for Valentine's yet, and anyway, I wouldn't want my roommate being murdered. Getting a good replacement would be problematic."

"Well, you might have to do that anyway if she marries one of them."

"Jodi. Please shut up. Please."

I then realized that Finn only knew about Gavin and not the mistake and letters from X. Damn, there was no wonder he'd worn a strange expression on his face.

"Oh, I forgot to tell you, Finn. There was a mix up. I got replies from two men, not one. Crazy, eh?"

"Hey, what if you ended up with both?" Jodi gasped. "How hot would that be?"

Finn looked from Jodi to me and back again. "Could I just pick up my suit and then escape away from this very uncomfortable girly conversation? Would that be okay?"

Jodi looked contrite. "Of course. My apologies, Finn. Come on through. I have some cookies from next door in my purse. Will you forgive me if I offer you one?"

"You didn't tell me you had cookies!" I protested.

"I'll bodyguard if I can eat yours as well," Finn said.

I narrowed my eyes at him. "Like I have a choice."

He grinned a triumphant grin before going through to the back.

The clock showed it was only 9:45 am. The time from now to when I would be able to write my next letters was going to take forever to pass, and then the wait for my final replies was going to feel like purgatory.

But soon, *soon*, I was going to get to meet my matches for real!

I wondered if either really was my future husband?

Chapter Nine

FINN

Jesus!

When Jodi raised the subject of Valentine's, I almost had heart failure. I thought they'd worked it out. But no, she just wants me to be her bodyguard.

I'm really hoping this isn't all going to backfire on me.

It's starting to feel like an amber alert weather warning.

Please don't turn red.

Chapter Ten

ELLA

I started my first glass of wine along with my first letter. The final one to Gavin. I didn't need Dutch courage for this one.

Dear Future Husband

Can you believe we're on our third letter already? Next is our blind date. I'm both nervous and excited.

Wow, you must write your own book. I'm sure you can do it. My roommate is a book editor. I'll

have to introduce you. I can't wait to hear about your story idea.

Maybe, given that we don't know what the weather will be like, we should make the candlelit meal with the classical music our first date?

I do like champagne by the way. I just didn't want you thinking I was a demanding diva hahaha.
Maybe we should go all out on our date?

Now, let me say this here. On dates I can pay my way. Romantic it may not be. Practical and fair it is. I insist, so now there should be no arguments over the bill when we meet.

You should also know this, the thought of eating seafood makes me want to hurl, so if it's okay please can you never eat it in front of me? I know it's a big ask but once, not too long ago, I had a dodgy prawn curry. Oh my, just writing about it here has me dry heaving.

I adore chocolate, so I hope there's a chocolate dessert on the menu.

Now I feel we've shared enough information for now.

Let's leave what happens on the date and after to fate shall we?

Ella xo

Looking over what I'd written to Gavin, I realized that actually I'd run out of steam with wanting to share any more information about myself. I'd be seeing him soon anyway. At least that's what I told myself, and not the probable truth, which was I was just so damn eager to write the letter to my mystery man!

I watched another episode of YOU while I drank a couple more glasses of wine. Then I opened up a fresh Word document and start the draft of my letter to Mr. X.

Dear Mr. X (Potential future husband)

Well, I have to say you surprised me too. But

then again maybe I like to be kept on my toes, (especially if it's because you've pushed me against a wall and I'm arching in ecstasy).

During the course of our meal, I will slip my foot out of my shoe and will lift it between your legs. My toes and the pad of my foot will slip and slide over your crotch, feeling your hardness as we enjoy our food. You'll watch me eat, being jealous of every morsel of food that goes into my mouth, wishing it was your cock, and for every sip of drink wishing it was your cum in my mouth.

On the drive home, the cab driver will believe he has the most perfect well-behaved couple in the rear as I sit back and still against my seat, refusing to touch you, to kiss you, until we are back in my home.

Every second of travel will bring you an exquisite agony of delayed gratification and by the time we exit the cab you'll want to run to my front door, and I won't be able to put the key in the lock quick enough (is that a euphemism?).

Once through the door, my shiny gold dress will be slipped off my shoulders until it lands in a pool at my feet.

You'll see my ass as I still wear no panties. My strapless nude bra will follow the dress until I am left in just my red heels.

This time it will be your turn and I will lead you to my bedroom where I will pull you down to sit on the edge of my bed, lowering your pants and revealing your erect cock.

You'll watch me lick around my lips before I take you deep. Right to the back of my throat. My tongue will swirl around your glans and I will suck, my fingers trailing over your balls. I will drive you to distraction until you come down my throat and I swallow every last drop.

Your shirt will come off next and I will sit on the bed and move astride your mouth as I demand my own satisfaction and ride myself on your tongue until I come.

By then you'll be ready for more and I will move

down your body and lower myself onto your cock, sinking you deep inside me, then letting you slide out, before sinking deep again. I will rotate my hips and work myself on your thick length, your hands kneading my breasts, our breaths harsh in the otherwise silent house.

You'll flip me over, having to show your alpha maleness. Pinning me to the bed, you will drive into me again, and again, and again, until I'm screaming your name and we both reach our crescendos. You'll gather me within your arms, and we will fall asleep.

It'll be like our souls entwined as well as our bodies.

Love, Ella xo

As I re-read the letter on screen, for the first time I wondered if I was making a mistake. What if I had just described a filthy fantasy to someone who turned out to be a complete pervert? What if I had zero chemistry with them and yet I'd written this?

Oh you've gone this far along with it. You may as well see it through to the bitter end. I told myself. I handwrite both the letters and mail them before I change my mind.

Finn comes in late. He was staying out more and more these days. I wondered if he had a girlfriend. The thought should have made me feel happy for him, but strangely it didn't. I missed him being around. God, I was stupid.

Chapter Eleven

FINN

As this shit storm drew nearer to its conclusion I couldn't sit still. I daren't be around Ella because she wanted to talk about the letters all the goddamn time. Instead, I was putting in stupid hours at the gym and going running. I may have told myself it was to avoid the apartment, but partly it was in case I ever thought fuck it and took her to bed, so she could admire my eight-pack.

Chapter Twelve

ELLA

Saturday, February 2, 2019

Another Saturday, another mail drop. My hair was grey with stress, I was sure. This had felt like the longest wait ever.

Inside was a letter from Grace herself, along with two more envelopes. The envelopes were both red this time.

Grace's letter read:

Dear Ella

I hope you've enjoyed the process of the What

The Heart Wants matchmaking service so far. Please find enclosed your final letters. Should you wish to proceed with a date with either (or both) of your potential matches, please email me at the usual address and I will set up your dates.

I have to say that usually I insist that letters to each other don't go into such graphic detail (wow, X's are scorching) but my gut feeling was that they needed to be passed to you as they were written, uncensored.

Anyhow, I believe the heart knows what it wants (hence the name of my agency), and I hope your heart finds its perfect match.

Love, Grace

She sounded such an amazing woman. I hoped her own heart found its match soon.

I opened the first envelope. This time it was X's. Inside was a Valentine's card. All it had on the front was a pink background and a large red heart and it said, 'Be My Valentine'. Inside it was blank except for his words.

Ella,

I hope we are indeed a perfect match and we
enact every single scenario we have described so
far. If not, it was a *pleasure* writing to you.

For your information...

The following morning, very early, I wake you
up having brought coffee to your bedside. You
smile up at me and I caress your cheek with the
tip of my fingers because although I am in lust
with you, I am also in love with you.

I climb into bed at the side of you and we
snuggle while you drink your coffee, and then
snuggles become caresses, and caresses became
heavy breathing, shattering orgasm touches,
and then finally exhausted, we fall back to sleep
in each other's arms until the alarm goes off.

Reluctantly, we part to go to our places of work,
but you spend the day with a delicious ache
between your thighs and every time you think
of us fucking a tingle happens and your panties
become damp. You wear a tiny little smile that

gives away the fact you spent the night in lust fueled endeavors. Throughout the day I text you about how horny I am, and I make witty comments like have you had a little prick (from your pins), and how you need to come home to me and my large cock. You'll joke you're coming home to a big prick.

So we'll meet back at the apartment and maybe we'll send for pizza and I'll let you choose which sort we have, but that way we can eat in your bedroom (the pizza won't be the only thing I'll be eating) and we'll only have to leave the room to answer the door, and other than that we can stay in bed all night.

Love, X.

That was it. My final words from X, who decided in the final letter to show me his heart after all. Next, I opened the second red envelope.

The card said: To my wife on Valentine's.

Seriously?

I stopped myself from being so judgy, and reminded myself that I started all this, addressing letters to my FUTURE HUSBAND.

I opened the card and read the verse.
True love comes to those who wait
And I have waited for you
Now it's almost time
Will you be my Valentine?
It was one of those cards you designed yourself, so he had made up the verse.
Inside he had written.

Dearest Ella,

Well, here goes. My final words. I have loved speaking to you in depth over the last few weeks, getting to know you inside, before the out. You are the most beautiful person and I really hope we are a match.

Whoever you end up with in life, Ella, they should count their lucky stars.

Hoping you arrange a date with me.

How wonderful would it be, to be able to tell our children that we met by writing love letters anonymously?

How truly romantic.
Gavin xo.

Oh wow. Actual wow. I had tears glistening in my eyes at his words, and I knew from my heart that I needed to meet both of these men. They both spoke to me from different viewpoints, but I had to know if one of them could be my actual perfect match in life. From their letters I couldn't choose between them.

I sent an email.

To: Gracegraham@whattheheart-
wants.com
From: Ellacassidy@yahoo.com
Date: February 2, 2019
Subject: Dates with my matches!

Good morning Grace!

I would truly like to meet both of the matches. Typical me, I'm afraid, but I can't decide.

What if I choose one, and the other was the love of my life?

Thank you for everything.

Kind regards.
Ella.

Later that day I received a reply.

To: Ellacassidy@yahoo.com
From: Gracegraham@whattheheart-
wants.com
Date: January 11, 2019
Subject: Dates

Dear Ella

As you know Valentine's Day is approaching and both your dates have requested that they meet you on this date. Gavin would like to take you on a lunchtime picnic, and he says he will cover the eventuality of potential inclement weather, and X would like to take you out to dinner. He has evening reservations for you?

Please let me know where they should meet you and at what time?

Grace.

I wrote back to Grace asking that both men gave me a place and time of where to meet them near to, or at where we would be eating. No one was getting my address until I knew I had chemistry with them.

Then I phoned Finn.

"Yo."

I let go the fact he was speaking like a teenager seeing as it was an emergency situation. "Finn, I have two dates for Valentine's."

"Greedy bitch."

"Be serious. It's the matchmaking thing. They both want to take me out on Valentine's Day. One at lunch, the other for dinner. I'm waiting to hear back about where they want to meet to eat. But can you still be my bodyguard, or have you got your own date?" I kept my fingers crossed he didn't have one.

"Ella, I don't have a Valentine's because I don't need a girl going all gaga goo-goo eyes at me and seeing all the proposals and telling me how lovely it is, and how they hope for that one day."

"What a prize for a woman you are."

"But are you seriously asking me to sit on my own in a restaurant on Valentine's day twice like some sad loser?"

The thought made me giggle. "That's hilarious. The icing on the top of the cake. You'll look like you've been stood up."

"Ha ha ha. Although, maybe all the female wait staff will feel so sorry for me they'll bring me free drinks and their phone numbers. It's on. I'll wear my new suit."

"The first date might be in a park."

"I'm wearing it anyway. For my bodyguard role. Don't spoil this for me."

"Okay. I'll let you know when. Where are you anyway?"

"Just getting changed from a workout. I'm all sweaty and naked while I talk to you."

"*Ewww, Finn.* See you later, and thanks."

Actually, I wished we were on videocall as Finn was a fittie. Eeek, I might get chance to get naked and sweaty with my own hunk soon.

Chapter Thirteen

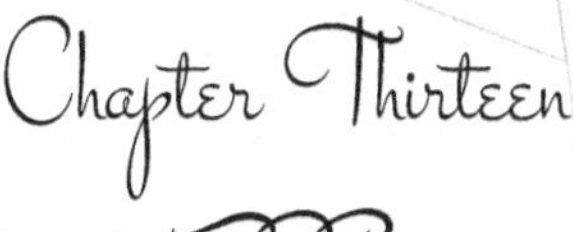

ELLA

Wednesday February 13, 2019

I was sitting in HappBEANness with Jodi, Casey, and Audrina. It was after closing and I had been ordered to come here so everyone could give me their opinions before my dates tomorrow.

"Okay, so what are you going to do if you meet Gavin at the entrance to Central Park tomorrow and you don't find him attractive?" Casey asked.

"I shall go and have the picnic anyway because it's the least I can do after he made so much effort, and anyway, I might still like him. Maybe his person-ality will shine through."

"And he could have a big dick." The voice came from the corner where Finn was sitting, having decided to work from the café for the afternoon. He'd said he may as well walk back with me and that he'd keep quiet, but I should have known better.

"Finn, mind your own."

"He's right though," Audrina said. "He could."

"Plus, you can't really ask Finn to keep out of it when you've asked him to actually go on the dates with you."

I turned to look at Finn's triumphantly smug grin and gave him the middle finger.

"No, babes, two dates, not one. That's the kind of guy I am. I'm there for you, for two dates."

"You're such a hero." I turned back to my friends.

"So what are you going to wear to the park? I'm guessing the gold dress is coming out for your fancy dinner. It's freaking stunning," Casey told the others. "She'll look like Cinderella did at her ball."

"I thought maybe black classic trousers and a white shirt? He's going to be reading poetry to me. I need to look learned."

Finn's voice boomed out once more. "You need a

massive warm coat because it's fucking freezing is what you need. Anyway, a guy won't care what you're wearing unless it's something showing a bit of leg, ass, or boob."

"Does anyone have duct tape?"

"Jesus, what are you planning on doing to them?" he quipped, ever the smartass.

"It's for your mouth, dickwad."

The others laughed. "Finn, I hope you're going to behave on Ella's dates," Jodi said. "They've been a long time coming and a lot of effort has gone in leading up to these."

"I'll be on my best behavior. I know they're special," he said.

We carried on drinking and chatting and then eventually, Finn and I walked the five minutes back to the apartment.

We walked along the hall and Finn spoke. "I'm gonna go straight to my room, Ella. I can feel a headache coming on. Probably eye strain."

"Oh no. Feel better soon. Anyhow, thanks for coming with me tomorrow. I feel safer knowing you're there."

"No problem."

I reached up on tiptoes to kiss his cheek. He turned to look at me and there was a moment's hesitation. A split-second where his mouth was oh so very close to mine and if either one of us moved just a centimeter...

He backed up. "See you tomorrow, Ella."

And with that, he was gone.

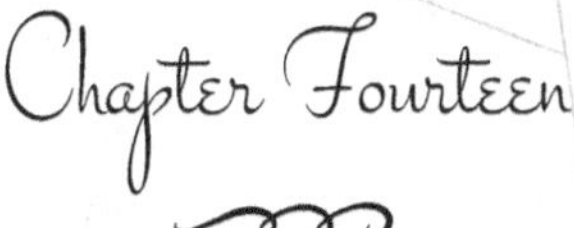

Chapter Fourteen

ELLA

Valentine's Day

I could barely work. I was a total mess all day. Luckily, it was quiet in the shop because most people had picked up their orders by yesterday. Jodi kept me in coffee.

For date one, I went for my classic look, but then I took Finn's advice too and brought a thick coat with me... and gloves.

Finn went completely overboard and hired a car so he could properly be a 'bodyguard', and so at twelve-thirty a suited Finn walked through the door.

My heart skipped a beat. I'd never seen him while

he was trying on his outfit and he looked sensational. Like some kind of movie star.

"I think unless your date looks like Henry Cavill, he's going to get an inferiority complex when he sees your bodyguard," Jodi whispered.

"Gavin won't see Finn. Finn will be sitting behind a tree or something."

"How do you live with that and not climb him like a tree?" She shook her head while wearing the look of disappointment of a teacher whose students haven't done their homework.

"Sshh. You're whispering really loudly," I scolded as I noticed the smirk on Finn's lips.

"Your carriage awaits, Miss Cassidy." Finn lowered his head and opened the door for me.

"Wish me luck," I told Jodi as I walked out of the door.

We waited at the entrance to Central Park for thirty minutes. "Perhaps he's at a different entrance?" I mused, while my heart thudded with adrenaline and my stomach whirred.

"No, you double-checked with Grace, it's this one," Finn assured me. "Look, send her a message telling her that you're in *Grayson's* across the street from Central Park. Come on, I'll buy you lunch."

I felt so disappointed. Part of me wanted to go home and cry, the other held out hope Gavin was just running late or was in hospital and hadn't stood me up.

"Come on. Grayson's does fantastic food."

"We'll not get in, it's Valentine's Day."

"Let's just see, shall we?"

Finn whispered to a waitress and she must have wanted in his pants because not only were we taken to a table, but it was a great table with a view of Central Park.

"Okay," Finn said picking up a menu. "Now, I know you have to leave if Gavin comes, but you're dressed up in your lovely classic outfit and I'm in a suit, so I think we should go for it, and do what the lovers do for Valentine's, okay? So, we're having champagne and that's final."

I giggled. "Okay, James Bond."

Finn ordered a bottle of champagne and then told me he could only have a small sip because he was driving.

"I'm only having one glass because I have my other date tonight—if they actually show up."

"Well, we'll take the rest back with us then," he said.

Finn had steak and I had a burger. We chatted and laughed, and I realized that my disappointment at Gavin's no show had lifted because I was enjoying myself anyway.

Finn insisted we had strawberries afterward and fed mine to me. He was such a dork. And then, he went into his pocket and took out a piece of paper. He knew everything Gavin had written to me as I had shown him. I wouldn't show him what X had written, but he knew and had made puking noises about what Gavin had wrote.

Unfolding the paper, he started to read out Keats' 'Sleep and Poetry'.

It was beautiful and I realized as I sat there that the reason I didn't care that Gavin was a no-show was because I'd fallen in love with my roommate.

In love.

I was *in love* with Finn?

OH MY GOD.

I. WAS. IN. LOVE. WITH. FINN.

I LOVED FINN!

"What's the matter?" Finn said, looking at my wide eyes. I felt like I was about to have a coronary alongside my realization.

"I just, I just—" I couldn't do it. What could I say?

"I just... realized I don't know if you have a middle name?" I blurted.

What the actual hell are you babbling on about, woman? A middle name?

Finn looked at me strangely. He put the paper back in his pocket.

He cleared his throat. "I do," he said. "It's Gavin. Finn Gavin Edwards."

"Oh my god, what a coincidence," I told him. "Can we get the bill now please?"

Finn sighed, but asked for the bill. I called Jodi. "My date was a no-show. Is it okay if I go home? I want to watch Bridget Jones or something before I try again tonight."

"Oh, honey, I'm so sorry. Sure, you go on home. Get yourself a pizza or something."

"Oh, I've eaten. Finn took me to Grayson's."

There was a pause. "But that place books three months out when it isn't Valentine's. How'd he get you in?"

"He's gorgeous and in a suit. He just smiled at a waitress and BOOM, best seats in the place."

"Right," Jodi replied.

As we got up to leave, I turned to Finn. "How much do I owe you?"

He shook his head. "You called me gorgeous. This is on me. My treat, okay?"

"Okay, thank you." My face heated. I had. I'd told Jodi he looked gorgeous. It was better I didn't speak unless necessary. I'd throw money on his bed later.

As I opened our apartment door, I heard a noise.

"Finn." I stood stock still. "There's someone in the apartment."

Rather than be scared, Finn just yelled out, "That little shit," and stormed in.

I followed him, taking my boots off on the way through and holding one in each hand in case I needed to throw them at the intruder's head. Instead, I found a guilty-faced guy who looked remarkably familiar, given that although he had a different hair color—his being dark blond—he had very similar features to the man I shared an apartment with. The blond-haired man had two shirts in his hand and two hangers lay abandoned on the floor.

"What have I told you about helping yourself to my clothes?"

"I'd have asked if you'd have been here. I have a hot date tonight, man. Help a guy out."

I looked from one to the other.

"Ella, meet my brother, Kit."

"And Kit has a key to our apartment?" I raised an eyebrow.

Finn looked guilty. "Yes, but only for *emergency situations*." He glared at his brother.

"It is an emergency. I have a hot date and no clean shirts."

Glaring at them both, I snarled. "Sort this out, and don't come in uninvited again, Kit." Then I softened my gaze. "Nice to meet you. But you call ahead in future. Okay?"

"Ooh, I can see why you stay here." I heard Kit say as I walked away, followed by the words, "Oof, what was that for?" and a growl of, "Shut up, already."

Chapter Fifteen

FINN

No sooner had I let Kit have a shirt and kicked him out did my phone ring.

"Hello?"

"Hey, Finn, it's Jodi."

"Oh, can you not get hold of Ella? She's here, let me get her for—"

"NO." She shouted that loudly, I had to hold my phone away from my ears. "It's you I need to talk to. *Gavin.*"

Fuck.

"How do you know?" I asked her.

"You just told me," she said with a triumphant tone.

"Fuck." This time I actually said it out loud.

"I had my suspicions when you miraculously got a lunch reservation and her date was a no-show. Then I thought about the suit and the car and I decided to pursue my hunch. How did you do it?"

"I emailed Grace and told her I thought I was Ella's perfect match. She agreed."

"And then what? It went wrong and she ended up with two matches. So how are you going to deal with the other one?"

"Erm, well, I'm going to pick her up from her apartment and well..."

"What? Drive her in the opposite direction of the restaurant?"

"Erm, no. I'm going to kiss her. That's the plan."

There's a stupefied silence from the other end and then the words, "Oh shit."

I wait for her next words.

"You're both of them, aren't you?"

I cleared my throat. "Yes."

"But why? Why two?"

"Because I wrote completely different things. She wanted romance, but I'm also a dirty bastard. So I gave her both. Then tonight my plan was to confess they're both me."

"She'll kill you."

"I have to take the risk. Being this near her all the time and not having her is killing me anyway. If it backfires, I'll just have to look for someplace else to live. I can't just be her roommate anymore."

"For what it's worth, Finn. I wish you all the best tonight."

"Thank you."

"I'll make sure you have a good send off after your death."

She hung up and a feeling of dread pooled in my stomach. I decided it was better to confess now and actually ask Ella on the date, than end up with her dream becoming a nightmare when her second date didn't turn out as she'd hoped.

Chapter Sixteen

ELLA

I sat back against my headboard disappointed at the no show. And I had no address so it wasn't like I could even write back and ask why. I could possibly ask Grace, but I couldn't bring myself to find the motivation. I had this other date tonight, and anyway, I'd realized I was in love with my roommate. God, I didn't even want this date anymore. I just wanted to do all those dirty things with Finn. It had been his face in my fantasies while I'd got myself off anyway. It was time I totally admitted to myself that my roommate situation was ruined. I couldn't stay around him while I wanted to do exactly what Jodi said and climb him like a tree. If he brought a girlfriend home, I might even punch them. It was no good. I was going to have to move.

Feeling maudlin, I decided to get the three letters out from Gavin and give them one last read before I ceremoniously burned them.

I picked up the first for the last time.

Dearest Future Wife

Thank you for your recent letter. I decided to wholeheartedly embrace your idea of conversing with you as a potential future partner!
Why not?

I'm Gavin, I'm twenty-eight, and I work in a library. I adore literature. Poetry, fiction, biography. You name it, I'm a fan. I do also enjoy movies, but I'd rather read the book if it's an adaptation.

Exercise wise, a stroll in the park sounds good. I do like to visit the gym a few times a week to keep myself in peak condition but also love fresh air.

I also have both my parents and I have an

annoying younger brother who is the same size as me in clothes and calls around to my apartment when I'm not there and 'borrows' them.

My ideal date would be a meal somewhere very romantic, maybe with a scenic backdrop, soft music and candlelight.

Is it too forward to say that I hope one day to be a father? At least one child but as many as makes my future wife happy. I hope I've not scared you away with that comment, but we seem to be saying we'll give these letters our all!

Music wise I like classical. If you play Taylor Swift, I shall forgive you (and wear noise cancelling headphones).

Hope to hear back from you soon.

Gavin.

I was smiling at finding out Finn's middle name was coincidentally the same when I re-read the bit about the younger brother and I froze. I started again at the beginning of the letter.

I work in a library. Finley Gavin fucking conning bastard Edwards did work in a library on occasion when he took his laptop there. He also **visited the gym a few times a week...**

Never. How could this be? Was FINN Gavin???

I hurtled out of my room and smacked right into a very hard chest.

Looking up I saw an extremely guilty looking face.

"Are you Gavin?" I asked. "Not middle-name Gavin, but romantic letter writing Gavin?"

"Funnily enough, I was just coming to tell you... erm, yes. Sorry, it's me."

I placed a hand on my hip. "And did you think this was an amusing joke?"

Finn vehemently shook his head from side to side. "No, I meant every word."

"You... you like me?"

"Yes, Ella. I do. A lot."

I held myself steady against the wall. "Fuck. I need some time to process this, okay? It's a lot to think about." My head was reeling.

"But do you like me too?"

I nodded. "Yes, I do. But I can't do this right now, okay? I need to re-read the other two letters from you, and then get ready for this date tonight."

His eyes searched mine. "You're still going on it?"

"Yes, it's not fair to cancel. At the very least I owe them a nice meal, even if I'm going to be turning them down. On Valentine's Day. I'm evil. The poor person."

His fingers gently moved to my chin and he tilted my face up to his. "You're not evil. You're lovely. I will do my bodyguard bit and then later, we talk, okay?"

I nodded again. It was all I was capable of right at that moment. "Okay."

We walked back to our own rooms. How the hell I managed to not run after him and beg him to take me to bed I had no idea, but I had principles and my manners said I need to be nice to X. Goddammit, I really loved his sexy words. He'd make a good writer. I was just sorry for him that I was in love with Finn.

Later, I stood at Finn's door dressed in my gold dress. Part of me considered wearing something else, but then I realized I wanted Finn to see me in it. I knocked on his door, but there was no response. Pushing the door open, I found he wasn't there.

He was supposed to be driving me to my date. *Where was he?*

A knock came at the front door. Sighing, I went to open it. To find Finn on the other side.

"Why are you knocking on our own door?"

He answered by pushing me back against the wall and capturing my lips with his.

Holy mother of God.

It couldn't be?

Never.

Could it?

He broke off.

"Are you X as well?" I asked on a husky whisper.

"Could be," he answered. "What would you say about it if I was?"

"I'd ask why you were talking when right now you were supposed to have your hand fisting in my hair and the material of my dress in your other hand."

We never made it to the restaurant after all.

Chapter Seventeen

To: Ellacassidy@yahoo.com
From: Gracegraham@whattheheart-
wants.com
Date: February 15, 2019
Subject: Happy Valentine's Day???

Dear Ella

I hope you can forgive me for the naughty subterfuge I engaged with, with Finn, in order to get you to your perfect match. I made him complete an application form and he was perfect for you, so I decided to

go along with his dastardly plans!
It was super fun, I have to admit.

Anyway, I wish you the very best and
hope you're very happy together. I'm
sure you will be. I'm amazing at
my job!

Love, Grace.

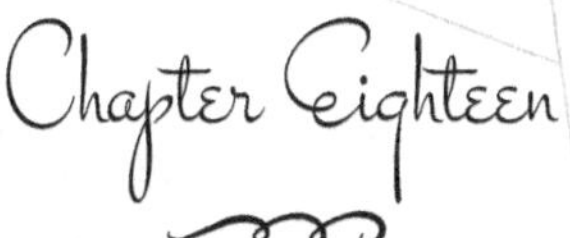

Chapter Eighteen

ELLA

I woke up as Finn brought me a coffee to bed. His fingers trailed up my cheek just like his letter said they would.

"Did you mean everything you said in your letters?"

"Yes. You need a room for your dressmaking, so I don't keep getting pins stuck in my feet. It's highly annoying."

I threw a cushion at him. "That's not what I meant."

He smiled. "I know, and yes, I meant every word. And I'm already halfway through writing my own book. It's about a man who has to live with the most irritating roommate ever and how he plots to kill her."

I narrowed my eyes at him. "As long as it's fiction."

He took my mouth with his and we enjoyed a long, leisurely kiss.

"So, what do we do next, dearest future wife?"

I laughed. "God, did it make you cringe that I wrote that?"

He lifted something out of his pajama pocket and dropped to his knees beside the bed.

"Ella Cassidy. I have lived with you for a while now. I know your faults and your dreams and I'm in love with them and with you. Would you do me the honor of becoming my dearest future wife?"

I had tears in my eyes and could barely speak.

"Seriously? This is not a joke?"

"It's not a joke, Ella. We can take our time, but you're mine. So what do you say?"

I nodded my head as tears rolled down my cheeks. "I say yes, Finn. I love you too. I say yes."

He placed the ring on my finger. It was slightly too large, but I didn't care. We could sort that later. Right now, I wanted the morning he promised in his letter.

Snuggles and sexy time with my dear future husband.

Who knew? He'd been right there all along.

139

THE END

To read the Keats' poem click here:
en.wikipedia.org/wiki/Sleep_and_Poetry

Harlow's story is next, *Together Forever*.

Acknowledgments

With thanks to my **Halo and Horns Reader Group** for assisting with coming up for a name for the coffee shop and to **Emma Causer** for the winning name HappBEANness. It's perfect.

About Angel

Angel Devlin writes stories as hot as her coffee.
She lives in Sheffield with her partner, son, and a
gorgeous whippet called Bella.

Newsletter:
Sign up here for Angel's latest news and exclusive
content, including a FREE short story prequel BAD
BAD BEGINNINGS.

geni.us/angeldevlinnewsletter

www.ingramcontent.com/pod-product-compliance
Lightning Source LLC
Chambersburg PA
CBHW022058050726

47591CB00002B/592